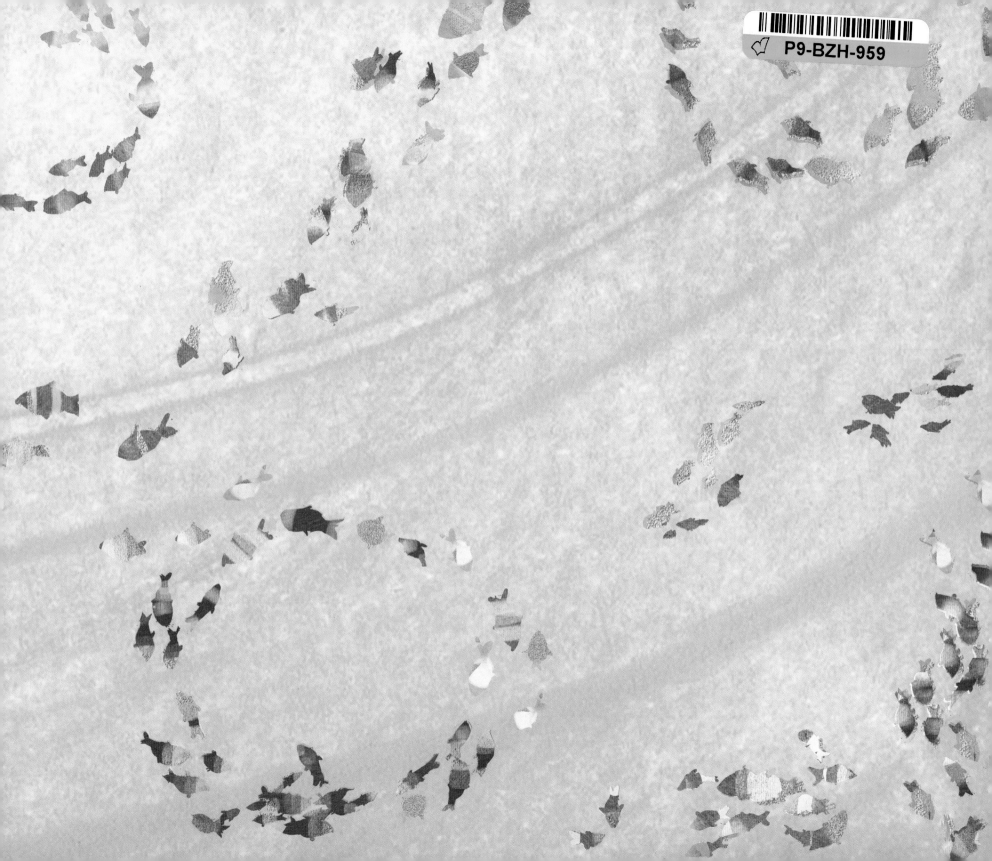

"What you seek is seeking you." –Rumi

For Olivia. –JV
To Jaska, Esme, and Peg,
an inspiring children's librarian. –MB

Text copyright © 2019 by Jacqueline Véissid.
Illustrations copyright © 2019 by Merrilees Brown.
All rights reserved. No part of this book may be reproduced in any form
without written permission from the publisher.

Library of Congress Cataloging-in-Publication Data available.

ISBN 978-1-4521-3780-3

Manufactured in China.

MIX
Paper from
responsible sources
FSC™ C008047
FSC
www.fsc.org

Design by Sara Gillingham Studio.
Typeset in Apéro.
The illustrations in this book were created
by digitally combining oil paint, relief print, and charcoal.

10 9 8 7 6 5 4 3 2 1

Chronicle Books LLC
680 Second Street
San Francisco, California 94107

Chronicle Books–we see things differently.
Become part of our community at www.chroniclekids.com.

CASPIAN
FINDS
A FRIEND

by Jacqueline Véissid · illustrated by Merrilees Brown

chronicle books · san francisco

Caspian lives in a lighthouse
surrounded by a cold gray-blue sea.

Every day, he watches the waves,
wondering, waiting, wishing for a friend.

Every night he casts his light out
into the darkness,

searching . . .

but no one arrives,
just the sea and the skies,

and so he waits.

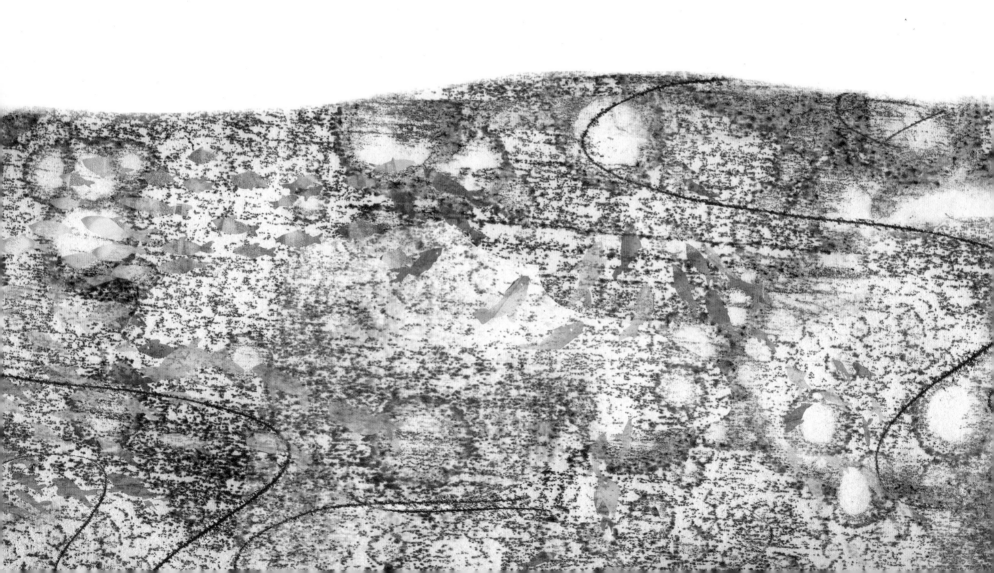

Until one day he has a new thought.
He hurries home to find paper and pencil.

On his table sits a bottle with flowers.

He empties it,

rolls up his paper,

and slips it inside.

Then down to the
wide open sea he runs
and throws the bottle in.

He watches it float away,

farther and farther,

smaller and smaller.

Days sink into weeks,
weeks into months.

He waits

and waits,

his hopes bobbing like a bottle on waves.

Early one morning, Caspian notices
a glistening nestled in the rocks.

He slowly uncorks the bottle
and pulls out a piece of paper.
Only one word is written.

He races to his little rowboat
and pushes out to sea.

Day fades into night,
and still he keeps rowing

and rowing.

The stars
shimmer to life,
illuminating
the darkness.

Caspian lies down in his boat and looks up—

watching,
　　wondering,
wishing—
　　and slowly falls asleep,
his dreams drifting on a gentle sea.

At first blush of dawn Caspian wakes.

In the distance he sees
something floating towards him.

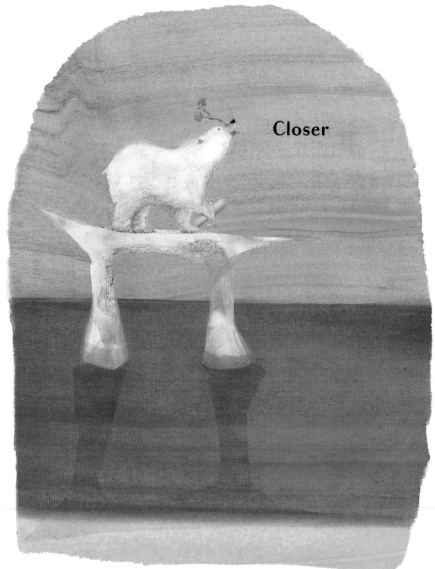

Closer

and closer.

Bigger

and bigger.

The bear's eyes are warm and gentle.
He slowly lifts up a piece of paper.

Will you
be my
friend?

Caspian holds up his.

Together they travel
across a sparkling sunlit sea,
back to the lighthouse,

back home.

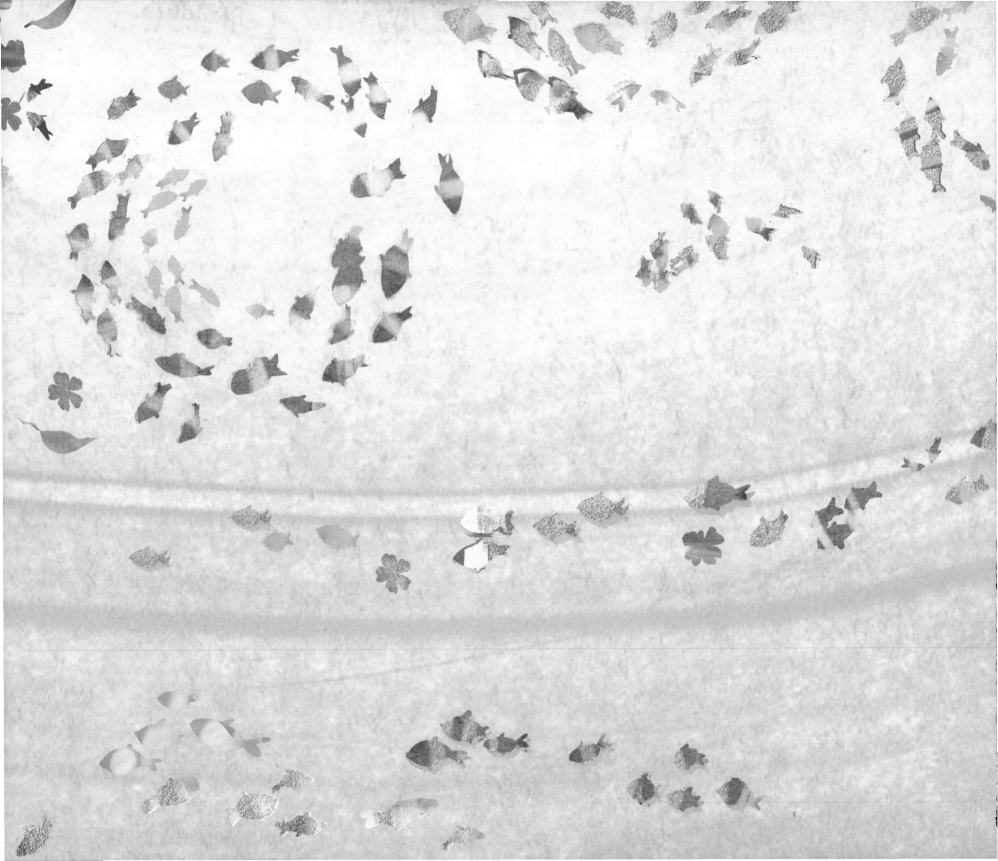